T0130265

The Adventures of Jeffrey

The Big Steal

MARYDITH KINGRY

ILLUSTRATED BY JAMES KOPP

© 2022 Marydith Kingry. All rights reserved.

No part of this book may be reproduced, stored in a retrieval system, or transmitted
by any means without the written permission of the author.

AuthorHouse™
1663 Liberty Drive
Bloomington, IN 47403
www.authorhouse.com
Phone: 833-262-8899

Because of the dynamic nature of the Internet, any web addresses or links contained in this book may have changed
since publication and may no longer be valid. The views expressed in this work are solely those of the author and do
not necessarily reflect the views of the publisher, and the publisher hereby disclaims any responsibility for them.

Any people depicted in stock imagery provided by Getty Images are models,
and such images are being used for illustrative purposes only.
Certain stock imagery © Getty Images.

This book is printed on acid-free paper.

ISBN: 978-1-6655-5797-9 (sc)
ISBN: 978-1-6655-5798-6 (e)

Library of Congress Control Number: 2022907750

Print information available on the last page.

Published by AuthorHouse 05/24/2022

authorHOUSE®

This book is dedicated to Sydney, Wyatt and Greyson.
May you always find the adventures in life.

eep, down in the clear blue water... from the depths of the central Florida swamps, lives a small hunter, who is crafty and intelligent... so well hidden by his surroundings that no human can find him. He is known as *Procambarus Alleni* to scientists, but you can call him...

Jeffrey!

"Hello!"

Jeffrey is a very special electric blue miniature lobster. One that lives an extraordinary life filled with adventure and fun.

Now Jeffrey isn't just your ordinary electric blue lobster. He is only 5 inches long. Jeffrey is an omnivore which means he loves to eat both vegetables and meat! Some of Jeffrey's favorite foods are zucchini, carrots, steak, and even hot dogs. Jeffrey also needs calcium to help him grow bigger and bigger.

Although he is orginially from the swampy waters of Florida, our electric blue lobster friend Jeffrey doesn't live in Florida, but with his human friends and their big dog Abby.

Jeffrey has a secret. A very big secret. A secret that he has never shared with anyone...Although Jeffrey is an ominivore that loves a variety of different foods, there is one type of food he truly craves... and Jeffrey dreams about this food every night.

Every night Jeffrey dreams about eating something very delicious. Something so delicious it is all that Jeffrey can think about... chicken!

Not just any type of chicken but oven roasted chicken! Not fried chicken. Not grilled chicken. Not even chicken parmesan. But a WHOLE golden, crispy, juicy roasted chicken. A roasted chicken so BIG it is even bigger than Jeffrey himself! But poor Jeffrey could only dream...

Then one glorious day Jeffrey woke from his daily afternoon lobster nap to the smell of...could it be? Could it truly be? Jeffrey was sure his electric blue miniature lobster nose could not be mistaken... roasted chicken!

But where was the delicious smell coming from? Jeffrey jumped out of his bed and looked out of his tank and around his human friend's kitchen. And what did Jeffrey see?

Not fried chicken.

Not grilled chicken.

Not even chicken parmesan.

But the chicken of his dreams, a whole golden, crispy, juicy roasted chicken!

A WHOLE chicken just sitting on the stovetop across the kitchen!

Jeffrey couldn't believe his eyes! He rubbed his eyes and looked again. What luck! A yummy, golden, crispy, juicy roasted chicken! And it was right out of the oven! This can't be! All of Jeffrey's dreams had come true!

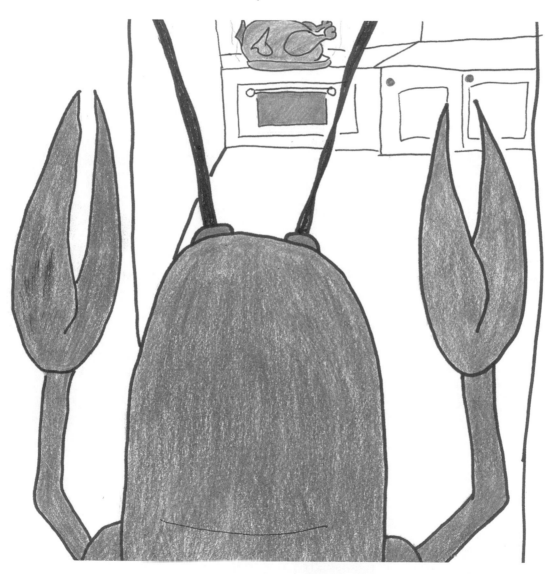

Oh! What to do? What to do? Thought Jeffrey...

And what was Jeffrey to do? How would a miniature electric blue lobster get across the kitchen to the hot, golden, crispy, juicy roasted chicken right in front of him? A perfectly plump and ready to eat golden roasted chicken.

But how was Jeffrey going to get that chicken? Could he get to the stove and get some of that scrumptious, golden, delicious chicken before his human friends came back?

Think Jeffrey, think!!!!

Jeffrey paced around and around in his tank, thinking. What WAS Jeffrey going to do? His dreamy golden crispy, juicy roasted chicken was right in front of him. Just then, Jeffrey's belly growled at the smell of that roasted chicken. Oh, the agony!

How could Jeffrey make his dreams come true? Poor Jeffrey!

Jeffrey thought to himself, I need to get some of that golden, crispy, juicy roasted chicken. Around and around Jeffrey paced...thinking, plotting, and dreaming of golden roasted chicken.

Now you may not know this about Jeffrey, but Jeffrey is incredibly handy and much smarter than your average electric blue miniature lobster from the depths of the Florida swamps. And for a miniature lobster like Jeffrey who loves fun and adventure, it didn't take long to come up with a perfect plan.

Just then Jeffrey snapped his claw! *Eureka!*

Jeffrey had an idea. And it was a very good idea. This was going to be an adventure of a lifetime!

"Ah-ha! Of Course!" Jeffrey thought to himself. He glanced around his tank for what he needed to put his plan in place and spotted his adventure chest. Jeffrey ran to his adventure chest and threw open the lid. Inside Jeffrey found his rope, a grappling hook, and his trusty parachute. All the tools an electric blue miniature lobster needed for the adventure of a lifetime.

Jeffrey packed up his adventure gear and laced up his shoes. Jeffrey had worked out the perfect plan, and he was ready to get that delicious golden, crispy, juicy roasted chicken of his dreams.

Jeffrey peered through the glass tank. He could see all around the kitchen. Jeffrey put his ear to the glass and listened carefully. The kitchen was quiet. The only sound he could hear was the humming of the refrigerator.

Jeffrey carefully popped open the lid to his tank and peeked out over the top.

Perfect opportunity! Not a human friend in sight! He tied his grappling hook to the rope and took a deep breath, and counted one, two, three, and jumped! As he sailed downward Jeffrey pulled the parachute cord and...

sailed safely to the kitchen floor. He peeked around to see if anyone had spotted him....

No!

Good!

He was safe! Jeffrey quickly moved across the kitchen as fast as his electric blue miniature lobster legs could go to the stove where that glorious golden, crispy, juicy roasted chicken was cooling.

Jeffrey took the rope and grappling hook from his shoulder fashioned a lasso, and threw it up into the air, landing it around the oven handle.

Jeffrey began to climb. And he climbed and climbed some more until he finally made it to the top of the stove. At the top, Jeffrey cautiously looked around to make sure no one was coming.

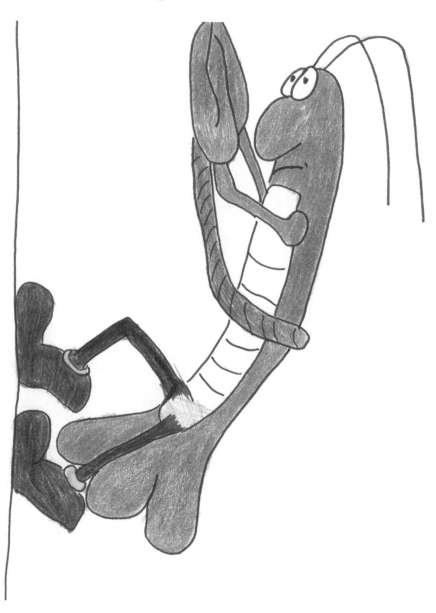

Jeffrey was so excited! He had made it across the kitchen and to the top of the stove! And right there in front of him was that whole golden, crispy, juicy perfectly roasted chicken!

But oh no! Jeffrey took a hard look at that big, golden, crispy, juicy chicken. The chicken was too big for Jeffrey to move on his own, and the whole chicken wasn't going to fit into his tank! Jeffrey worried that his human friends would catch him eating his chicken at any moment... and then what? No more chicken for Jeffrey!

Jeffrey had to make a decision! And make one quick! Jeffrey looked at the chicken again and decided. He would have to settle for the drumstick. A whole big, hot, golden, crispy, juicy drumstick!

Jeffrey quickly cut the drumstick off the chicken and tied it to his back with his homemade lasso.

Boy, was that drumstick heavy for a electric blue miniature lobster! But there was no way Jeffrey was going to leave that drumstick behind. He had come too far to give up now on the juicy chicken meal of his dreams!

But oh no! What was that?

All of a sudden, Jeffrey could hear the voices of his human friends in the other room. It sounded as if they were coming towards the kitchen! Jeffrey looked around for a place to hide. He looked at the butter dish... no that wouldn't do! It wasn't big enough to hide his drumstick... He could run behind the flour bag. No, that wouldn't work either.

Just then, Jeffrey looked down and saw that the family dog Abby had curled up for a nap on the kitchen floor. Jeffrey suddenly had another great idea! He grabbed his parachute, closed his eyes, took another deep breath, and jumped!

Jeffrey parachuted down and landed on Abby's back! Abby yelped as she was startled by Jeffrey and took off running across the kitchen with Jeffrey on her back.

Oh no! thought Jeffrey. Jeffrey held on as tight as he could as Abby ran around the kitchen at full speed! Abby rounded the corner, and as she ran past Jeffrey's tank, Jeffrey lept off Abby's back and grabbed onto the edge of his tank.

Jeffrey hung, dangling by a claw! Jeffrey wasn't about to give up now! He pulled himself up to safety with his hard earned juicy drumstick tied tightly to his back.

Safely back at his house, Jeffrey carefully lowered the drumstick into his tank. He climbed back into his tank and put away his tools in his adventure chest leaving behind no trace of his escapade to the kitchen stove.

Jeffrey set the dinner table and put on his good dinner bib. Exhausted from his adventure, he finally sat down to enjoy the golden, crispy, juicy roasted chicken he had always dreamed about while savoring every bite.

With the drumstick picked clean, Jeffrey's tummy was full of hot golden, crispy, juicy roasted chicken dinner.

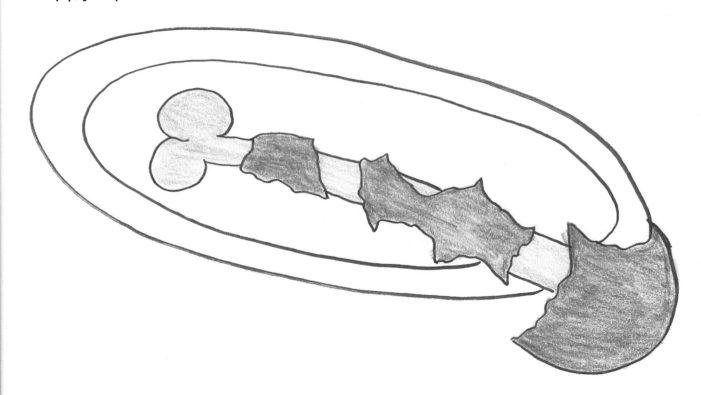

Jeffrey suddenly was very tired and felt sleepy. After all, for a very special electric blue miniature lobster, it had been an adventurous day! Jeffrey yawned and climbed into bed to get a very well-earned good night's sleep. As Jeffrey slept, he dreamed about his next adventure and where it would take him in the big world, just outside his tank.

Printed in the United States
by Baker & Taylor Publisher Services